Jerry Dooty extended his cupped paws. "I found these on the floor in Maureen's office."

We leaned closer. He held a bunch of little-bitty pieces of wood. Headless matchsticks.

"I thought they seemed a little . . . I don't know, suspicious?" he whined. "Figured I'd take them to Principal Zero, see what he thought."

Natalie frowned. "You think he'll think she's suspicious?"

"I think he'll think she's not thinking," said Mr. Dooty. "Maybe he'll think she made the stink."

"The stink?" I snapped. "You think?"

"I think." Jerry Dooty gave an elaborate shrug. "But who cares what I think? I'm just the assistant janitor."

Could he be right? Could my mongoose pal have sunk so low? I shook my head. Never in a million lunchtimes.

Mr. Dooty shuffled past us, droning, "But I'll tell you one thing—"

Before he could finish his one thing, three things happened.

First, Natalie sneezed. "Ha-CHOO!"

Second, an eerie creaking, like the front doors to a thousand haunted houses, filled the air.

And third, with a loud FOOMPF! the one-story building next to us collapsed.

Chet Gecko Mysteries

And don't miss

Dial M
for Mongoose

FROM THE TATTERED CASEBOOK OF

CHET GECKO
PRIVATE EYE

Bruce Hale

sandpiper

Houghton Mifflin Harcourt
Boston New York

www.hmhbooks.com

The text of this book is set in Bembo.
Display type set in Elroy.

The Library of Congress has cataloged the hardcover edition
as follows:

Hale, Bruce.
Dial M for mongoose / by Bruce Hale.
p. cm. —(A Chet Gecko mystery)
Summary: Fourth-grade detective Chet Gecko and his associate Natalie Attired
investigate a series of mishaps that all seem to point to the school janitor.
[1. Geckos—Fiction. 2. Animals—Fiction. 3. Schools—Fiction.
4. Janitors—Fiction. 5. Humorous stories. 6. Mystery and
detective stories.]
I. Title.
PZ7.H1295Di 2009
[Fic]—dc22

ISBN: 978-0-15-205494-6 hardcover
ISBN: 978-0-547-48079-4 paperback

Manufactured in the United States of America

DOC 10 9 8 7 6 5 4 3 2 1
4500263563

To MJ Wong, a true-blue Gecko supporter.

A private message from the private eye . . .

I wonder about things. Like, if corn oil comes from corn, where does baby oil come from? If people from Poland are called *Poles*, why aren't people from Holland called *Holes*? And why is it that writers write, but fingers don't *fing*?

That's what detectives do. We wonder. (Others wonder how I manage to stay in school, but that's a subject for another time.) I'm Chet Gecko, finest lizard detective at Emerson Hicky Elementary and two-time former yo-yo champion.

Mr. Ratnose wishes I was even half as curious about schoolwork as I am about my cases. But you can't have everything. (And if you could, where would you put it?)

Lately, I've been wondering more than usual. Especially about this: How well do you really know the folks you know?

My investigations often show me the seamy underbelly of school life, but this case threw me for a loop. Folks I thought were the salt of the earth turned out to be the scum of the pond. And low-down punks turned out to be nice guys.

It's enough to make a gecko give up detecting and start knitting doilies. (Just kidding. I can't knit.)

But it took everything I had to tough out this case. Through fear and fire and thefts, I kept digging for the truth like a mole tunneling to Mumbai.

And why? Loyalty, pure and simple.

Someone was trying to put my mongoose janitor pal Maureen DeBree on ice. And a true-blue PI doesn't take that kind of monkey business lying down. (Standing up, maybe.)

Against all odds, I followed the tangled trail of clues to a conclusion that was nuttier than a squirrel's sundae and riskier than a playdate in a piranha's swimming pool.

But in the course of my investigation, one thing rang true: When you want your floors waxed, dial *M* for mongoose. But when you want danger, deception, and mysteries unraveled, dial *G* for Gecko.

1

The Big Stink

You can't avoid it. No matter what, at some point in every school day, during that long, long stretch between lunch and freedom, time stands still. The great wheel grinds to a halt, the universe holds its breath, and the birds forget to sing.

Everything stops.

Except Mr. Ratnose's mouth.

That drones on and on and on, explaining the layers of the earth's crust, the eight parts of a plant, the ten types of clouds, the workings of friction, the wonders of the water cycle, the principle of gravity, and the true, exact meaning of the phrase, "bored out of your ever-lovin' skull."

This stretch of frozen time is also known as "science lesson."

Nothing against science, but I'd rather investigate the mysteries of a case than the mysteries of molecules any day.

Halfway through this one particular science lesson, I glanced at the clock. Sure enough, the minute hand hadn't budged for at least an Ice Age.

Would this day never end?

Then, from the nonstop *blah-blah-blah* at the front of the room, two words penetrated. The sound of my name.

"Chet Gecko?" said Mr. Ratnose. "That's the twelfth time you've checked the clock in the last minute. Is there somewhere else you'd rather be?"

Such an easy straight line.

I muttered, "Um, at the dentist, running from rhinos, shopping for underwear . . . Did you want the full list?"

Mr. Ratnose scowled. His response felt like an old line from an even older movie. "Go to the attitude adjustment corner," he said wearily. "Maybe that will teach you some manners."

"Maybe," muttered my friend Bo Newt, "but I doubt it."

"How's that?" said Mr. Ratnose.

I sighed. "Uh, I said I'm on it." Past the desks of stupefied students I shuffled, back to the dusty corner and its pink plastic chair.

"You'd better be, mister," said Mr. Ratnose. "Parents Night is Friday, and I'm telling *your* parents everything." But even his warning had a kind of been-there, done-that feel to it.

I slumped into the chair, facing a poster of Rodney Rodent in a rocket that read YOUR ATTITUDE DETERMINES YOUR ALTITUDE.

If Rodney was right, I was on the fast track to Lower Nowheresville. I hadn't had a new case in weeks, my wallet was flatter than a tapeworm's tummy—heck, I even had time to do all my homework. (Not that I actually *did* it.)

If this kept up, I'd turn from Chet Gecko, Private Eye, to Chet Gecko, Regular Guy. I was hungry for something, anything, to break the boredom.

But I wasn't ready for the Big Stink.

I sat quietly, practicing my thumb twiddling—forward twiddle, reverse twiddle, fast, medium, and slow—when the whiff of a funky stench tickled my nose. Craning my neck, I searched for a culprit in the back row.

No shifting in seats. No telltale fake innocence. All my classmates looked like bored little angels.

The stench grew stronger. I fanned the air in front of my face. "Whew."

A giggle erupted from somewhere close at hand.

3

"He who smelt it, dealt it," whispered Rick Shaw, a nerdy hedgehog.

The giggling grew louder. Now several of the back-row kids had turned around to stare and point.

I shook my head. "Wasn't me."

"Sure," said Rick. "*We* believe you."

Then the funky stench cranked up another couple of notches, from cheese-cutting to paint-peeling. It seemed like it was coming from the direction of the wall. Poor wall.

"Oh, man." I stood and backed away.

Mr. Ratnose's lecture droned on. But by this time, the odor had tiptoed on its little stink-footed feet throughout the class. More and more kids were turning and searching for its source.

Finally, even Mr. Ratnose noticed me. "Chet Gecko, why did you leave your seat?"

"Smells like he blasted himself out of it," said Waldo the furball. "Hur, hur."

"It wasn't *me!*" I repeated.

Now the class laughed uncontrollably. Some of the nearer kids got up and scooted back.

Mr. Ratnose put a fist on his hip. "Settle down, class."

I covered my nose. "I think it's coming from over near the vent."

"What is?" Mr. Ratnose asked. Then the stench wave hit him. "Oh. Sweet Norwegian pie! What *is* that?"

Somewhere along in here, the class finally realized this stench was way beyond anything one kid could have caused. More and more of my classmates were on their feet, moving back from the heating vent.

I joined them.

"Oh, *baby*," cried Bo Newt.

"That *stinks!*" said Shirley Chameleon.

"Hoo-*eee!*" said Waldo.

How can I describe the intense odor? It was the pharaoh of funkiness, the sheik of stenchiness, the grand high pooh-bah of putrid. In the ranks of rank smells, it would be head honcho of the whole dang enchilada.

And all I wanted was to leave it behind. (No pun intended.) Luckily, Mr. Ratnose agreed.

"Class!" He coughed and waved his hand. "Out—*kaff kaff!*—side!"

We were way ahead of him. By the time he finished speaking, everyone had jammed into line and was pushing through the doorway. Out in the hall, other classes milled around, eyes watering, noses covered.

It wasn't just our stink. Every classroom in the school was emptying out.

"Terrible!" cried Bitty Chu, teacher's pet. "Think of all the class time we're missing." She held her nose.

"Wonderful," I said, breathing deeply. "A fresh mystery—*koff!*—at last."

2

The Mark of Zero

I was champing at the bit to start investigating the Big Stink. But Mr. Ratnose had other ideas.

"Everyone stick together," he said. "To the playground!"

Other teachers must have had the same thought. We all tramped out onto the grass in cheerful, well-organized chaos, like an anthill on a field trip.

I took advantage of the confusion to locate my partner, Natalie Attired.

Along with the rest of her class, she was following her teacher, a tough turtle named Ms. Amanda Reckonwith.

"What's the word, mockingbird?" I called.

She turned and raised an eyebrow. "You mean, what's the stink, rat fink?"

"Exactly," I said. "*That's* what I want to know."

Natalie was a sharp-looking mockingbird with an even sharper tongue. Some say she put the *smart* in *smart aleck*. I'd go a step further. With her common sense and puzzle-solving skills, I'd say she put the *wise* in *wisecracker*.

"This smell reminds me of something," she said. "Something that's brown and sounds like a bell."

"What's that?" I asked.

"Dung!" She cackled.

Cancel that *wise* comment.

Taking her by a wing, I said, "Let's go find Principal Zero."

She planted her feet and stared at me like someone who had just brought a bug-eyed alien to the Spring Fair. "You're actually *looking* for trouble?"

"No, for a case. Maybe he'll hire us to find out who stinkbombed the school."

"Class," barked Ms. Reckonwith. "No talking!"

When she cracked the whip, the students clammed up in a hummingbird's heartbeat.

Natalie glanced at her teacher. "Maybe later," she whispered.

I shoved off. My class was still milling about. Time to make my move.

Mr. Zero stood at the edge of the grass, talking with two teachers. He was a hefty pussycat with a wacky taste in ties and a reputation for chewing out his students' patooties like so many packs of bubble gum.

His reputation was well deserved.

"Heya, boss man," I said. "How's tricks?"

His amber eyes frisked me, while his tail lashed gently from side to side. "Gecko," said Mr. Zero. Somehow, coming from his mouth, it sounded more like "Yuck-o."

"Need some help getting to the bottom of this stench?" I asked.

"When I need help, I'll ask for it," he rumbled. "And not from some fourth-grade, two-bit gumshoe."

I put a hand to my chest. "That smarts, chief. After all we've been through? At least give me a shot at it."

The corner of his mouth lifted, revealing an ivory fang. "As it happens, Ms. Shrewer is already on the job. And here she comes now."

Vice Principal Shrewer trudged up the hallway, taking off a gas mask. She was a hard-bitten shrew with an expression as sour as stinkbug-and-vinegar yogurt.

"Well?" said the big cat. "What was it?"

"Carelessness, pure and simple," said Ms. Shrewer.

"How do you mean?" I asked.

Both administrators turned to eyeball me. "Is this any of your business?" said Mr. Zero.

"No," I said. "But a gecko could *make* it his business."

The principal pointed a sharp claw. "A gecko could also go *out* of business."

I shrugged. "There's no business like . . . no business."

They resumed their conversation.

"Anyway, I searched the boiler room and found a jumbo jar of ammonia by the heating vent," said the shrew.

"Ammonia?" I said. "But—"

A look from Mr. Zero silenced me. "Ammonia alone wouldn't cause that smell," he said.

"No," Ms. Shrewer agreed. "But it looked like someone had accidentally dropped some match heads into the jar. *That's* what caused the odor."

Match heads in ammonia? A classic stinkbomb. That wasn't an accident; that was planned.

Mr. Zero stroked his whiskers. "Any idea *which* someone is responsible?"

"Isn't it obvious?" said the shrew. "Who else uses ammonia around here? Maureen DeBree."

"Ms. DeBree?" I said. "But she'd never—"

"Gecko," Principal Zero snapped. "Zip it and ship it."

I bit my lip. Something was rotten, and it wasn't just the funky smells drifting across campus. I wanted to snoop some more, but the big cat had spoken.

"Later, administrator," I said.

Mr. Zero growled, deep in his throat.

"I mean, administrator, *sir*." I beat a hasty retreat.

As I headed across the playground, thoughts chased through my head like overheated penguins after an ice-cream truck.

Maureen DeBree was our neat-freak janitor, a big-hearted mongoose with a thing for Mr. Clean. She'd helped me out of many a jam—like the time she'd saved me from a pair of king cobras who had a serious attitude problem.

I knew our janitor. And I knew that she'd be more likely to fly off to Neptune with a nene goose than to set off a stinkbomb.

As I rejoined my class, Ms. DeBree reached Principal Zero's side. Even a blind gecko could tell he was giving her a tongue-lashing for the ages.

The mongoose protested. She waved her hands about, and her face looked like Hurricane Agnes on a bad day.

Clearly, Ms. DeBree hadn't done the deed. But who had? And why?

After all the times the janitor had saved my bacon, my mission was clear. It was time for me to return the favor.

Later, I'd wish that I'd thought twice before jumping into Ms. DeBree's mess.

But later, of course, would be too late.

3

Loosey Mongoosey

The rest of that day's lessons were as pointless as a plucked porcupine. We camped on the grass and pretended to pay attention, while the janitor and her assistant rounded up enough electric fans to de-stinkify the vents and the classrooms.

By the time they'd finished, school had ended.

Natalie and I hung around until our fellow students cleared out, then we hoofed it over to Maureen DeBree's office.

Banging and rattling echoed from halfway down the hall. It grew louder as we approached her room.

Was the janitor in trouble?

"Marggin' argle barg snarfn bargin'!" Someone inside was cursing a blue streak. (Either that, or they were speaking Lithuanian backwards.)

Natalie and I burst through the open doorway.

"Are you all right?" I cried.

Ms. DeBree sat on the floor, surrounded by what looked like all the cleaning products in the known world—jars and canisters, bottles and brushes, sprays and scrubbers, and some items I had never even seen before.

"Uh, Ms. DeBree?" said Natalie.

"Aha!" cried the mongoose, plucking a canister from the pile. "Just as I deflected: The buggers stole my ammonia."

"How's that?" I asked.

"See?" said the janitor, holding up the stinkbomb jar next to her own bottle. "Mine has the gold seal on the label. I always get the extra-strength kine." She took a deep whiff of the open jar and closed her eyes. "Ahhh. The best."

Natalie and I exchanged a glance. Word around the school yard was that Maureen DeBree took her cleaning products seriously. I didn't know she took them *this* seriously.

"So you're not responsible for that stinkbomb," I said.

"That's what I'm tryin' for tell you," said the mongoose. "Some punk kids did 'em. But I don't know how they broke in here and stole my stuff."

14

I whipped a business card from my pocket. Fancy lettering arched over crossed swords, a skull, and two bundles of dynamite.

The cards were a gift from an admirer. An admirer, coincidentally, with the same name as me.

Handing it to the janitor, I said, "Maybe we can help."

"Nice dynamite," she said. "But I don't need no help."

"Why not?" asked Natalie. "Principal Zero looked pretty mad."

The mongoose waved a paw. "It's all a case of forsaken identity. He'll cool down. No sweat."

"No sweat?" I said. "He accused you of accidentally stinkbombing your own school. You cleared the air. Don't you want us to clear your name?"

"Nah," said Ms. DeBree. "When I show the boss these bottles, he'll change his tune."

This wasn't going quite as I'd planned. She was supposed to hire us to investigate. She was supposed to end my boredom.

"Please?" I said.

The mongoose chuckled and showed us to the door. "Thanks, but no thanks, Mr. Private Eyeball. Go run along and detect something else, 'kay?"

"The only thing *he's* got to detect are the answers to his homework problems," said Natalie.

"Don't remind me, birdie," I said.

We shuffled off down the hall. But I had a funny feeling that this case was only just getting started.

Or maybe it was just the aftereffect of the bean-and-beetle burritos I'd had at lunch. Sometimes it's hard to tell the difference.

The next day, Ma Gecko hustled me and my deeply annoying little sister, Pinky, off to school well before classes started. Normally I don't do early mornings. But Ma Gecko had a convincing way of making her case. ("Get your tail in gear or lose it," I believe were her exact words.)

Sunrise found me stumbling past the flagpole and through the school gates. Pinky peeled off to do whatever it is that first graders do. I made my way to the lunchroom.

If I played my cards right, the head cafeteria lady, Mrs. Bagoong, might part with a fresh-baked spittle-bug muffin or a slice of banana-slug bread. It was worth a shot. After all, the early morning shouldn't be a total waste, right?

Dew sparkled on the grass like sunshine on a teen's brand-new braces. Out on the playground, the swings hung limp. Only a handful of kids roamed the halls. The school was quiet, peaceful.

But when I stepped through the cafeteria doors, that peace was shattered like a cut-rate piñata at a fullback's birthday party.

"You know you did it, and if you had a shred of decency, you'd admit it!" Mrs. Bagoong shouted.

Fists clenched, she stood toe-to-toe with Maureen DeBree. The hefty iguana towered over the janitor, but Ms. DeBree held her ground.

"You're one lolo lizard!" she snapped.

I hotfooted it over to them before fists started flying.

"Whoa now, ladies," I said. "What's the squawk?"

Mrs. Bagoong pointed a finger like a salami. "She left the door unlocked."

"And *she* is dreaming if she thinks I done that," said the janitor.

"So why the fuss?" I said, pushing between them. "I've left plenty of doors unlocked."

The queen of the lunchroom swept an arm toward her monster-sized refrigerator, which hung open. "*That's* why the fuss. Someone came in last night and cleaned out most of my veggies. Now what will I serve?"

"No veggies?" I said. "I thought this was something serious."

"It *is* serious!" cried Mrs. Bagoong. "Kids will be missing out on my newest recipe: broccoli-and–lima bean pie."

One look at her scowl told me this wasn't the time to mention that nobody in their right mind would miss it if she never served those two vegetables again.

"How do you know Ms. DeBree left the place unlocked?" I asked.

"Because." The lunch lady planted a hand on her hip. "I locked the doors when I left yesterday, and she always comes around later for the final check."

Maureen DeBree stuck her furry muzzle in Mrs. Bagoong's face. "And I told you, when I checked 'em, they was locked."

I held up my hands. "Hang on. Maybe somebody busted in."

"I looked," said Mrs. Bagoong. "No sign of it. The culprit just waltzed through the door."

The janitor crossed her arms. "Well, it wasn't *my* fault."

"We'll just see about that," said the big iguana. "I'm going to tell Principal Zero." She slammed the fridge and stomped out through the open doorway.

"Oh, yeah?" Ms. DeBree called after her. "Me, too!"

I caught her arm. "Wait, before you go . . ."

"Yeah?"

"Sure you don't want to change your mind about hiring me?"

The lean mongoose looked across the room, bit her lip, and nodded. "Yeah, yeah, okay. You're hired, Mr. Private Eyeball. See if you can learn who's tryin' for make me look like one incontinent mongoose."

"Yes!" I said, breaking into a victory jig.

Ms. DeBree raised her eyebrows.

I stopped and slapped on a serious expression. "I mean, uh, *yes,* I'll find out which low-down punk is trying to make you look incompetent. That'll be seventy-five cents for a retainer."

"That's highway robbery!" said the janitor.

"No, that's the cost of justice," I said. "And cheap at twice the price."

She shook her head and dug into her pouch for the quarters.

I couldn't suppress my grin. A case at last!

Oh, foolish detective.

4

Jerry Dooty

I gave the kitchen a quick once-over, but didn't see anything suspicious.

Maureen DeBree filled me in as I walked her up to the office. There wasn't much filling to do. She didn't know how the punks had stolen her ammonia, and she hadn't left the cafeteria unlocked. Period.

But she did pass me a couple of leads.

I left her at the admin office door. Having seen Mr. Zero in action once or twice before, I wasn't eager to repeat the experience.

Down the hall I skipped. Her cool coins jingled in my pocket. Then I caught myself—hard-boiled private eyes don't skip.

I turned my feet toward Ms. DeBree's office and

my first interview. Mystery was in the air.

Halfway down the corridor, the public-address system crackled. Mr. Zero's voice boomed, "Paging Chet Gecko. Your fly is open."

I started to glance down, then caught myself.

A familiar cackle echoed off the wall. Those mockingbirds sure can mock.

"Nice try, Natalie," I said. "But any flies around me would be history."

She dropped off the roof of the covered walkway and glided to a landing. "Wanna hear my Mr. Rat-nose?"

"Cut the comedy, birdie. We've got a case." I ran down what little I knew about Maureen DeBree's troubles.

She cocked her head. "Are you sure the two things are connected?"

"No, I'm not," I said. "That's why they call it investigation—we investigate and find out."

"Oh, really? If you're so smart, why don't you do your homework more often?"

"Funny," I said, "that's what Mr. Ratnose says."

She smoothed her wing feathers. "And what do you tell him?"

"It's a mystery to me." I led the way to the mongoose's office and rapped on the door. "Mr. Dooty? You in there?"

After a long pause, the door creaked open. A glum-faced gopher peered out. "Yeah?"

"You must be Jerry Dooty?" I asked.

"I suppose I must," he said. "Nobody else wants to be."

The assistant janitor was a small gray gopher, as unremarkable as an old wad of gum under a desk. His yellow teeth poked out between chubby cheeks like candy corn between two mounds of pudding. If Jerry Dooty were a doormat, his message wouldn't be *Welcome,* but *Go ahead—everyone else does.*

I stuffed my hands in my pockets. "Can we ask you some questions?"

"Oh, sure," the gopher whined. "Everyone knows my time's not worth anything. I've got nothing better to do."

He slumped against the doorframe.

"So," I said, "how long have you worked with Maureen DeBree?"

The gopher shrugged. "A month, maybe. Seems like forever."

"Is she pretty easy to work for?" asked Natalie.

"Just swell." Mr. Dooty crossed his arms. "If you like working, which I don't."

I scratched my tail. This guy was so depressed, he made Eeyore look like a cockeyed optimist.

"Has anyone got a grudge against her?" I asked.

A noise like a hyena choking on a wax banana came from Jerry Dooty's mouth. It might have been a laugh.

"Maureen?" he said. "Everybody likes her. Some people are all sunshine and unicorns and daisies. Not me, boy. Nobody likes me."

"I'll trust you on that," I said.

Natalie cleared her throat. "Moving right along . . . Do you have any idea who might have set the stinkbomb or unlocked the cafeteria?"

The assistant janitor's chin sunk lower. He scratched his nose forlornly. "Me? Nobody tells me anything. I must be the least popular worker at school."

"No ideas at all?" I asked, slumping. His mood was beginning to affect me.

The gopher brushed at his drooping whiskers. "Ever think she might have done it herself? You know, accidentally?"

Natalie cocked her head. "Ms. DeBree, the queen of clean?"

He shrugged again. "I'm just saying she's been sloppy lately, not herself. But fine, don't believe me. Nobody ever does."

"Thanks for the tip," I said, with a grimace. "Uh, we've got to get back to Happy Land."

"Oh, sure," said Jerry Dooty. "Nobody likes spending time with ol' Jerry."

Natalie waved. "Have a nice day!" she chirped.

"Never have," the gopher mumbled as he closed the door. "Wouldn't know what to do with one if I did."

When we were well away from the janitors' office, I stopped and shook myself all over. "Yeesh. Get a load of Mr. Sunshine."

"You said it."

"I've got to do something to throw off his mood, or I'll be down all day."

Natalie arched an eyebrow. "A swing on the swings?"

I smiled and pulled out Ms. DeBree's change. "And a Pillbug Crunch bar. Just what the doctor ordered."

After a treat and a swing, I was ready to tackle anything. But wouldn't you know it? The bell rang. All I could tackle was math lessons.

I blew out a sigh and headed off to class. It wasn't fair. All the other detectives filled their days with secretaries and secret messages and mysterious clients. What did I have? A bad case of Mr. Ratnose.

At least there was one small mystery to toy with. Rick Shaw, the hedgehog, was absent and nobody knew why. Illness? Sudden family trip? I suspected terminal nerdiness.

"Nobody's seen Rick Shaw?" asked Mr. Ratnose. "It's not like him to miss school."

If you asked me, ol' Rick had picked the right day to skip out.

A couple hours of cruel and unusual punishment later (also known as decimals, division, and vocabulary test), I would have hung up my school career, given half a chance. I settled for recess instead.

Natalie was waiting for me beneath the scrofulous tree, our usual meeting spot. "What a *magnificent* day!" she said. "I'm *partial* to *pursuing* detective *procedures* on a *splendid* day like today."

I rolled my eyes. "Someone aced her vocabulary test."

"My *achievement* was *outstanding*." She beamed and fanned herself with her wing feathers.

"Okay, Webster. Let's *suspend* the, uh . . . show-offishness and get to work."

"Didn't do so well yourself?" she asked.

"I don't wanna talk about it." I led the way across the playground to our next interview. "Ms. DeBree said she'd had some run-ins with the Dirty Rotten Stinkers in the past. How shall we play this?"

Natalie offered a tight smile. "How about not at all?"

The Stinkers were the school's worst gang. Their ranks bulged with thugs, lugs, punks, skunks, and plain old no-goodniks. They were the rancid cheese in the triple-decker silverfish and sauerkraut sandwich that was Emerson Hicky Elementary.

"Aw, c'mon, Natalie. It won't be that bad."

"Not bad?" she said. "Do you remember the time you fingered them for vandalism, so they tied your tail in a knot and buried you in a Dumpster?"

"Harmless hijinks," I said, strolling toward the portable buildings. "Besides, it's ancient history. I'm sure they've forgotten about it by now."

We rounded the corner of the first building and saw the Dirty Rotten Stinkers: Erik Nidd, killer tarantula; Bosco Rebbizi, bad-tempered ferret; Kurt Replie, no-account rat; a wart-covered toad whose name I didn't know; and a half-dozen other mugs.

All eyes stared at me.

"Chet Gecko," said Erik, flexing four of his eight legs. "Ya got a lotta nerve comin' around here."

Natalie gulped. "What were you saying about ancient history?"

5

The Power of Positive Stinking

The original tarantula bad boy, Erik Nidd, crawled toward us like a tank—if a tank had eight hairy limbs, a chip on its shoulder the size of a pyramid, and a really nasty disposition. His beefy arms and legs bulged with muscle, and his many eyes glowed with cruel delight.

"Gecko and bird," he said. "How nice. We wuz just lookin' around for someone to cream."

In spite of myself, I took a half step back, then turned it into a dance shuffle. "Cream? No thanks. I like my coffee like I like my girls."

"Strong and pure?" said Natalie.

I turned to look at her. "No, not at all. Yuck."

"Enough fancy-pants talk," said Erik. He flexed

his other four legs. "Let's do some clobberin', Stinkers."

I edged closer to the building. "We didn't come here for a clobbering."

"Where do you usually go?" Miss Warts-a-lot, the toad, hopped closer.

Natalie cleared her throat. "We came to ask some questions," she said.

Erik's face crinkled in puzzlement. "Questions?"

"Yeah," I said, "like, what is the capital of Venezuela?"

"Uh," said Erik.

"What is the average airspeed of a common loon?" asked Natalie.

"Well . . . ," said Bosco, the ferret.

"What's twenty-four times seventy-three?" I said.

"Um," said Miss Warts-a-lot.

Natalie leaned in. "And what's the best way to make a stinkbomb?"

The tarantula broke into smiles. "Oh, *that's* easy. Ya take a big ol' jar of ammonia, drop in a bunch of match heads, and seal it up for a week."

"Exactly," I said. "Oh, one last question."

"Yeah?" said the toad.

"Did you Stinkers set that stinkbomb yesterday?"

"We—" Miss Warts-a-lot began.

The ferret cut her off. "Cheese it. We ain't telling you nothin', peeper."

Erik Nidd growled, "Question time is over. Now it's playtime."

At his signal, the other Dirty Rotten Stinkers started closing in on us.

"What are we going to play?" said Natalie. "Rock-star Hero? Chinese Jump Rope? Duck, Duck, Goose?"

Bosco grinned. "How 'bout Pound the Peepers?"

Natalie and I backed up. "Strange," I said, "but I don't think we like the same games."

"Get 'em, ya mugs!" cried Erik.

"Yahhh!" shouted the Stinkers.

Natalie and I whirled. She flapped wings and I beat feet away from there as fast as we could go. We tore across the playground.

"Maybe they're only trying to put a scare in us," said Natalie.

I glanced back. The thugs were close behind, snarling and snapping.

"Nope," I said. "They really do want to cream us."

We zigzagged around the crowded sandbox, and cut through a football game, hoping to shake them. No luck. They stuck with us like ugly on an ape.

Only one solution.

"Who's on yard duty today?" I asked Natalie.

"Ms. Glick, I think," she panted.

I spotted the hefty alligator. "Perfect."

"Come back here, ya twerps!" cried Erik Nidd, scrambling in pursuit.

"I think not," I said.

We dashed past a jump rope game and up to Ms. Glick.

"Well, well," rumbled the gator. "Natalie Attired and Chester Gecko."

I hate when they call me by my full name.

"Uh, hi, Ms. Glick," I said. "What's cookin'?"

The teacher eyed the pack of Stinkers, who skidded to a halt and pretended to be deeply interested in Double Dutch.

"Trouble, as usual," she said. "And I bet you're at the heart of it."

"Me?" I said. "I'm as innocent as the day is long."

"Uh-huh," said Ms. Glick. "A midwinter day in Greenland, maybe."

She gazed at us. We stared at the Stinkers.

The gang showed no signs of moving along. In fact, the little rodents skipping rope got nervous, and *they* beat feet. The Dirty Rotten Stinkers just stood in a knot, muttering and glaring.

"Since you both seem so fond of my company," said Ms. Glick, "perhaps you'd like to see pictures of my trip to Florida." She pulled out a photo album from a handbag the size of an aircraft carrier.

I glanced over to Erik, who mouthed, "You're

dead." I looked up at Ms. Glick. "We'd be delighted," I said.

You haven't really tasted boredom until you've spent most of your recess pretending to admire photos of alligators in lounge chairs and leisurewear. At long last, the Stinkers drifted off like a foul breeze. The coast was clear.

Natalie and I said a final "Mm, nice beach" and bid farewell to Ms. Glick.

Skirting the edge of the playground, we chewed over what we'd learned.

"You think they set off the stinkbomb?" said Natalie.

"Definitely."

She cocked her head. "But how can you tell the Stinkers are guilty?"

I shrugged. "They're breathing?"

"I'm serious," she said. "How can you be sure?"

We stopped beside a krangleberry bush.

I scratched my chin. "They practically admitted it. Besides, my gut tells me so."

"I thought your gut told you, 'Eat that bag of katydid crisps.'"

"Sometimes it does," I said. "This time it says they're guilty."

Natalie groomed her wing feathers. "And are they guilty of stealing the food, too?"

"I dunno. My gut doesn't say."

Natalie rolled her eyes.

I pointed across the grass. "Hey, here comes our client."

"And she doesn't look happy," said Natalie.

That was an understatement. The janitor looked bluer than the only Chihuahua on a Saint Bernard snow rescue team. Her bright eyes were dull, and her bushy tail drooped.

"Hey, Ms. DeBree," I said. "Why are you draggin' your wagon?"

She shuffled up to us. "It's even more worser than I thought."

"What is?" said Natalie.

"Mr. Zero put me on notice," she said. "He thinks I'm gettin' sloppy."

"What?" I said. "Why?"

The janitor sighed. "Seems like the veggies wasn't the only thing that went missing last night."

Natalie leaned closer. "What do you mean?"

"Somebody sneaked into the office and did some embuzzling," said Maureen DeBree.

"You mean . . . ?" I said.

"They stole the cash box."

"Sweet jumpin' jellyfish," I said.

The mongoose nodded. "And you ain't whisperin' Dixie."

6

Take It or Thieve It

This was getting out of hand. Literally. Suddenly it seemed like anything not nailed down at Emerson Hicky was fair game for the thief. I needed to learn more about him.

"Same M.O.?" I asked.

Maureen DeBree lifted a shoulder. "How should I know whether the creep had stinky armpits?"

I shook my head. "Not *B.O.*, *M.O.*," I said. "It means *mo* . . . uh . . . it means how they did it. Don't you ever watch TV cop shows?"

The mongoose gave me a mournful look. "No break-in," said Ms. DeBree. "The bugger came through the door, just like at the cafeteria."

"Are you sure you remembered—" Natalie began.

"Yeah, I *checked*," huffed the janitor. "The office door was locked. Cheez, don't you trust your own client?"

I held up a hand. "Of course we do. Just being thorough."

Maureen DeBree halfheartedly picked up a stray candy wrapper. "Ain't this the straw that broke the kangaroo's back," she muttered. "Like I don't have enough on my mind already."

"What do you mean?" Natalie asked.

"Huh? Oh, I get more worries than Mr. Zero giving me the ax."

"Do tell," I said.

Ms. DeBree toyed with the wrapper. "Some bugger's been piling dirt out past the playground, making a mess. Our electricity bills are sky high, like someone's tapping into our power grid. And some of my buckets and wheelbarrows have walked off."

"Wait a minute." My tail twitched. "You mean to tell me your dirt's dumping, your bill's jumping, and your barrow's bumping?"

The mongoose gave me a glum look. "Yeah."

"Why didn't you mention this before?"

"You didn't ask," she said.

Natalie paced. "Any idea who's behind it?"

"Nope," said Ms. DeBree.

"Any idea if all these things are connected?" I asked.

"Unh-unh," said the janitor, watching the candy wrapper float down into a trash can.

"Hmm," I said.

"Hmm," Natalie agreed.

"For real." The mongoose shuddered. "This whole thing gives me the oodgie-woogies. Who would wanna do this to me?"

"Wait a second," said Natalie. "Why should Mr. Zero blame the office theft on your sloppiness?"

"Yeah," I said. "After all, anyone could swipe a key and steal the loot."

Ms. DeBree shook her head. "Nobody's key went missing, and the principal trusts all his office staff. Besides I *am* the last one to check the locks every day."

"Fear not, fair mongoose," I said. "We'll prove you innocent. In fact, we'll jump right on it and—"

Brrrrinng! The class bell cut me off.

"Investigate at lunch," said Natalie.

Dang. Schoolwork sure gets in the way of being a big-time detective.

Lunch that day was crab spider cakes and tick taco salad, with mango maggot bars for dessert. How do I remember these things? I am, after all, a trained detective. (Also, I had seconds.)

Mrs. Bagoong was still surly about the veggie theft. I was still relieved.

After a final belch, I sailed my tray onto the dirty stack and headed out with Natalie to clear Ms. DeBree's name. We stepped onto the grass, and I stopped short.

"Hey, I just had a brainstorm," I said.

"Good," said Natalie. "Maybe it'll wash out your ears."

I pushed my hat back. "We've been looking at this all wrong."

"Should we be squinting?"

"Instead of trying to figure out why someone's got it in for the janitor," I said, "we should figure out why someone's stealing and stinking up our school."

"You think the culprit isn't trying to make Ms. DeBree look bad?" said Natalie.

"I don't know," I said, striding across the grass. "But I do know this: We need to rustle up some other suspects than just Erik Nidd, PDQ."

"Pudgy, dim, and quirky?" said Natalie.

"Pretty darned quick," I said.

As we walked, I surveyed the busy playground. Things looked normal enough. Two basketball games raged on the blacktop. A group of older girls played soccer. And just beyond us, some third-grade bowlers were using grasshoppers as pins and pill bugs for balls.

Say what you will about Emerson Hicky, we've got all the major sports covered.

"See anything suspicious?" said Natalie.

"No," I said. "Wait—who's that?"

Over near the fence, a furry mug in a yellow construction hat was spreading a pile of dirt. He stood out like a tank in a sandbox.

"Search me," said Natalie. "I've never seen him before."

We legged it over to the stranger. He was a tough-looking mole with a nose like an exploded eggplant and paws like a pair of catcher's mitts.

I cleared my throat. "'Scuse me, chief."

"Whaddaya want?" he barked. "I'm a busy guy."

"We're, uh, the Welcome Wagon," said Natalie. "And we want to welcome you to Emerson Hicky."

Eggplant Nose gave us the once-over. "Oh yeah?"

"Yeah," I said. "I'm Chet Gecko, and this is Natalie Attired. We haven't seen you around before, so we, uh, wanted to welcome you."

"So?" he said, glancing back at his dirt mound.

"So, welcome," said Natalie.

The mole narrowed his eyes. "You said that already."

I tried my Number Five Friendly Grin. "What's your name, friend?"

"Nunya," he said.

"Nunya?" said Natalie.

Eggplant Nose crossed his arms. "Yeah. Nunya business. Now, get lost."

"Are you working for Ms. DeBree?" I asked.

His jaw tightened. "Look, bub, I'm an independent contractor. Workin' for the firm of Beatit, Buzzoff, and Scram. Get it?"

"Got it," said Natalie.

"Good," said Eggplant Nose. He went back to spreading the dirt.

We left the mole to his work and ambled onto the playground.

"Friendly fella," I said.

"You think he's hiding something?" said Natalie.

I shrugged. "A heart of gold and a sunny disposition? Maybe. It's no crime to be a grouch, but still . . ."

"We should keep an eye on him," said Natalie.

"Agreed," I said. "But we're using *your* eye."

7

Clues Blues

For the rest of lunchtime, Natalie and I wandered about, searching for clues. (Pretty much the same way I approach my homework.)

The office held nothing of interest. No muddy paw prints, no busted windows, no dropped library cards with the culprit's name on them.

"What *are* you looking for?" asked Mrs. Crow, the secretary.

"Anything that tells us how the thief got in here or who he was," I said, peeking under a stack of papers.

Natalie leaned on the counter. "Who's got office keys?"

Mrs. Crow counted off on her wing feathers.

"Let's see . . . Mr. Zero, Ms. Shrewer, the nurse, the janitors. Five altogether."

"What about you?" I asked.

"What *about* me?" said the crow.

"Don't you have a key?"

Mrs. Crow shook her sleek black head. "Hon, I practically *live* here. Who needs a key?"

We gave up on the office and hit the cafeteria.

It, too, looked as shipshape as ever. And when we checked out the boiler room after that, no red-hot clues reared their little heads and shouted, "Here I am! Notice me!"

If the same someone was stirring up all these different kinds of trouble, he'd covered his tracks well.

Lunch wound down like a grumpy preschooler at bedtime. Natalie and I ended up on the playground, kicking around a soccer ball and some half-baked notions.

"Could the Dirty Rotten Stinkers be behind it all?" asked Natalie.

"Nah," I said, lining up a shot. "They're not bright enough to snatch the cash box without breaking down a door or two. And stealing veggies?"

I booted the ball and it went wide.

Natalie smirked. "I get your point. Erik Nidd and broccoli don't exactly go together like worms and caramel." She flapped after the ball.

I grimaced. "I'm not sure worms and caramel go together. But you're right there, partner. The stinkbombing has their fingerprints all over it, but we've got no solid proof."

"So who's behind the rest of it?"

She hauled off and punted. The ball bounced off my chest with a *whump*.

I staggered back. "I dunno. Jerry Dooty?"

"Too depressed to steal much of anything," said Natalie. "How about Eggplant Nose?"

Showing off my fancy footwork, I retrieved the ball. "He's mean enough. But what's his motive?"

"I don't know. But something about him isn't quite right."

"What?" I swung my leg. The ball sailed into a krangleberry bush.

"I just said I don't know." Natalie picked her way through the shrubbery.

A nearby squirrel called to us. "Hey! If you're not going to play soccer with that thing, why don't you give someone else a try?"

"Because," I said, "this is how we get our kicks."

Lunch ended and schoolwork resumed. Through the next couple of lessons, I puzzled and puzzled some more (and occasionally even thought about my lessons). Although we had our suspicions, Natalie and

I lacked enough evidence to pin the crimes on anybody.

That meant we needed more info.

But what? And from where? I needed a clue, a lead, an inside tip.

What I got was more grief from Mr. Ratnose.

"Chet Gecko," he said, "let's hear your book report."

"Teacher, you really don't want to hear my book report."

He folded his hands on his desk. "I most certainly do."

"You won't like it," I said.

Mr. Ratnose sighed. "Which book is it?"

I stood and put my hands behind my back. "*The Wonderful Wizard of Odd,* by L. Frank Barmy." I paused.

"Yes?" said Mr. Ratnose. "Tell us all about it."

"Well . . . there's this wizard, see? And he's, uh . . . kinda odd."

My teacher stared at me for a long moment. "You haven't actually read it, have you?"

"Well, I . . ."

He held up a hand. "Never mind."

I sat down. "Told you you wouldn't want to hear it."

At long last, recess arrived. I rushed out the door

with my classmates to savor the sweet, sweet air of freedom.

How was I to know it would soon be full of dust?

Natalie and I began by investigating the snack machine. I cleverly detected a bag of Skeeter Pieces and we polished it off in short order.

All sugared up and ready to rumble, we pointed our tootsies toward our client's office. Maybe she had some more leads for us. (Or at least some more quarters. I'd already burned through her retainer.)

As we headed down the hall, Jerry Dooty was walking up it. Oddly, his paws were cupped together.

"What's up, Mr. Dooty?" I said.

The gray gopher turned his bleak gaze on us. "You're asking the wrong guy. I haven't been 'up' since Moses was in knee shorts."

"Uh, right," said Natalie. "So, what have you got there?"

"Evidence," he said. "Remember I told you Maureen was getting sloppy?"

I nodded. "Yeah?"

He extended his cupped paws. "I found these on the floor in her office."

We leaned closer. Jerry Dooty held a bunch of little-bitty pieces of wood. Headless matchsticks.

It wasn't like Ms. DeBree to leave anything on the floor of her office—not even footprints.

"Where are you taking those?" I asked.

"I thought they seemed a little . . . I don't know, suspicious?" he whined. "Figured I'd take them to Mr. Zero, see what he thought."

Natalie frowned. "You think he'll think she's suspicious?"

"I think he'll think she's not thinking," said Mr. Dooty. "Maybe he'll think she made the stink."

"The stink?" I snapped. "You think?"

"I think." Jerry Dooty gave an elaborate shrug. "But who cares what I think? I'm just the assistant janitor."

Could he be right? Could my mongoose pal have sunk so low? I shook my head. Never in a million lunchtimes.

Mr. Dooty shuffled past us, droning, "But I'll tell you one thing—"

Before he could finish his one thing, three things happened.

First, Natalie sneezed. "Ha-*CHOO!*"

Second, an eerie creaking, like the front doors to a thousand haunted houses, filled the air.

And third, with a loud *FOOMPF!* the one-story building next to us collapsed.

8

Cold Hard Crash

Natalie and I staggered, caught in a sudden whoosh of air like the breath of a giant. Blown sideways, we cried out. "Yaahhh!"

Our yells turned to coughs.

A huge cloud of dust billowed out, as if a million chalkboard erasers were being clapped by a half million teachers' pets. Bits of wall and roof rained down.

Natalie and I collapsed onto the grass, hacking like a couple of cats with major-league hairballs. Slowly, slowly, the dust settled.

I rose on my elbows and squinted through the fog.

Beside me, Natalie had gone all white, like a snow sculpture of a mockingbird. She lifted her head.

"That's one heckuva sneeze, partner," I said.

She spat dust. "Who *nose* what really caused it?" Natalie blinked. "Hey, where's Mr. Dooty?"

I scanned the scene but nobody showed through the cloud.

"Mr. Dooty!" I called.

"Are you all right?" shouted Natalie.

For a long moment, nothing stirred.

Then a shape slouched through the fog—an all-white gopher. "This is going to be *so* much work," groaned Jerry Dooty.

"Was anyone inside when it went down?" asked Natalie, getting up and shaking herself off.

The gopher removed his cap and whapped it against his leg, raising puffs of dust. "Why does the worst stuff always happen to me? I have awful luck."

"He's still in shock," I told Natalie. "Let's go check it out."

We edged closer to the pile of rubble, poking here and there. I thought I saw a lean animal, like a weasel or ferret, bound through the far side of the dust cloud. But when I blinked, it was gone.

"Hello?" said Natalie.

"Knock, knock," I said, rapping on a piece of lumber.

Her eyes twinkled. "Who's there?"

I gave her a look. "Me, birdie."

"Me, birdie who?"

"Natalie, not everything is a knock-knock joke."

"Says you."

At that moment a crowd of kids came running from the playground. They gaped and chattered and pointed.

We rummaged some more. Luckily, the ruined building was deserted.

Principal Zero and Maureen DeBree arrived at the same time. Both of them converged on us, talking over each other.

"What happened here?" said the principal. "Gecko, were you involved?"

"Chet, Natalie, you okay?" said the janitor. "Who did this?"

"Was anybody hurt?" said Mr. Zero.

Brushing dust off my sleeves, I answered, "The building fell down, no, yes, I dunno, and no."

"Don't worry, chief," said Ms. DeBree. "I'll get to the bottom of this."

The big cat's fur stood up like nerds volunteering for computer duty. "You'd better. One more slipup around here, and I'm hiring a different head janitor. School safety comes first."

"That's not fair!" I said. "How could she be responsible for this?"

Mr. Zero planted one thick paw on his hip. "Fair? Fair is pony rides and first kisses and cotton candy."

"But—" Ms. DeBree began.

"*I'm* responsible for running a school here," said the principal. "You're responsible for buildings and grounds. And you two . . ."

"Yes?" Natalie asked.

"Should be getting an education and staying out of my way," said Mr. Zero. He stomped past us, tail twitching.

"Oh, well," I said to myself. "One out of two ain't bad."

Natalie grinned. "*One?* Who says *you're* getting an education?"

Ms. DeBree and Mr. Dooty roped off the wreckage with CAUTION tape, called in a couple of badger contractors, and went to work. I love work. I could sit and watch other people do it all day. But just when they broke out the big tools, the class bell rang.

Back we trudged to face the humdrum drudgery of the only kind of work I don't care for: school-work.

After class ended, Natalie and I dropped by the rubble to get the scoop from our client. The two janitors were loading the last of the debris into the back of a truck. The badgers were hauling off a Dumpster. Two more Dumpsters stood nearby, stuffed with more junk than a greedy kindergartner after Halloween.

"So what's news, mongoose?" I said.

Ms. DeBree paused and wiped grime off her forehead with a spotless handkerchief. "It's one mystery, for sure," she said. "The wood is good, the floor seemed solid, but somehow it all collapsed into a hole."

"Weird," said Natalie.

The mongoose scratched her head. "Yeah. Almost

like we built the building over a hole and it finally fell in." She shook herself. "But that's cuckoo."

Natalie and I climbed down into the crater that used to be a classroom. Nothing to see but a hole. Hard to detect much from that.

We scrambled back out.

"Hey, that hole reminds me of something," I said.

"Your grades?" Natalie smirked.

"Nope, that digger." I went over to Ms. DeBree, who was loading a last chunk of wall into the truck. "Did you hire a bad-tempered mole in a hard hat to clean up around here?"

Her eyebrows drew together like two caterpillars crossing swords. "A mole? No . . ."

Mr. Dooty slapped his forehead. "Oh, I'm such a dum-dum. I forgot to tell you. Mr. Zero asked me to get someone to haul off the dirt piles, like I don't have enough to do around here. Was that okay?"

The mongoose nodded, but her face stayed as glum as the last kid to be picked for the softball team.

"Cheer up," said Natalie. "Look on the bright side."

"What bright side?" said the janitor, stepping into the truck cab.

Natalie waved a wing. "We've already had a

stinkbomb, two thefts, and a classroom cave-in. What else could go wrong?"

What else? Only a foolhardy detective would ask *what else?* And unfortunately, that's exactly what we were.

9

Hot Friggety Frog

The next morning, things at Emerson Hicky were quiet but tense, like a classroom where nobody's done the homework and the teacher's asking for volunteers.

No fresh thefts, no exploding Dumpsters. But the whole school seemed to be holding its breath. Word of the latest happenings had spread, and students and teachers were looking over their shoulders.

My old pal, Bo Newt, was absent. Nobody knew why. Was this something sinister, or just a day of playing hooky?

"Where's Bo?" I asked Bitty Chu. "Is he sick? It's not like him to skip school for anything less than a circus or a skateboarding festival."

"Why should *I* care?" she said. "He's a smart aleck."

"Yeah, but he's *our* smart aleck."

I brooded about my missing pal. And the knowledge that Parents Night was coming the next day didn't help my mood any.

At recess, only the little kids carried on with the same gusto as usual. Natalie and I tried to rustle up some clues, but we were as luckless as the only chicken at a fox family reunion.

"Could the Stinkers have tunneled under that classroom?" I asked.

Natalie preened her shoulder feathers. "Not their style. And can you picture Erik Nidd trying to dig with all those legs?"

"Good point."

We eased along the edge of the grass.

"What about Jerry Dooty?" said Natalie.

"What about him?" I scanned the clumps of kids engaged in soccer, tetherball, and quiet conversations.

"He *is* a gopher," said Natalie. "Maybe *he* undermined the building."

"So he could clean up the mess he made? *Bzzzt*—I'm sorry, wrong answer."

Natalie touched my arm with a wing tip, stopping me. "Okay, hotshot, I know where we might get an idea who sunk the classroom."

"Where?"

She pointed to Mrs. Crow, who was waddling up the hallway. "*She* knows which teacher's classroom collapsed. Maybe that teacher can give us a lead."

"Mrs. Crow!" I called. "Can we talk?"

She narrowed her eyes. "What's in it for me?"

Before I could tell her, fate got in the way—again.

With a loud *ka-whompf!* flames burst from the next building down the hall.

The sprinklers above us exploded into action with all the enthusiasm of an un-housebroken puppy, soaking the three of us to the skin.

Ring-ah-ring-ah-ring-ah-ring! The fire bell blared.

"This flippin' school," said Mrs. Crow, hunching her shoulders against the spray. "What's next? A rain of cockroaches?"

I took her wing. "This way!"

We squished out onto the grass.

"I'll go get Mr. Zero," said Natalie. She spread her wings and flapped off.

"I suppose I should tell the fire department which building is burning," grumbled Mrs. Crow. She pulled a cell phone from her fat red purse and waddled off, tapping buttons.

What did that leave for me? The dangerous stuff.

I edged closer to the blaze. Pure heat beat against my face and body, like I was stepping into an oven (and one without fresh cookies, to boot).

"Hello!" I shouted at the two-story building. "Is anybody in there?"

No response.

"Hello? Anyone?"

Still no answer. Maybe all the students were safely out on the playground. For once, things would go the easy way.

I glanced behind me. Kids stood at a safe distance, gawking. Nothing like a blaze for break-time entertainment. Might as well waltz on over and join them.

I had almost reached the group. Then I heard a sound that chilled my blood.

"Helpity-help-help!" someone cried. It came from the building.

"Who's that?" I shouted.

"It's—*koff!*—mu, mi, mo, me!" It sounded like a dame. I knew of only one dame who talked like her sentences had gone through a blender set on *mixed-up*.

"Popper?" I called. "Where are you?"

"Inside the—*koff koff!*—clickety-clockety-class-room!" cried Popper. "I'm stickety-stuck!"

Dang and double dang.

I scoped out the high windows of the burning building. They were open, and flames crackled from two of them. Smoke poured from a third. And in between those billows, a yellow-green froggy face peeked out.

Popper.

"Hang on, short stuff!" I yelled. "I'm coming!"

I tugged off my soaking-wet trench coat and wrapped it around my shoulders and face. Then I beat feet, straight for the inferno.

Fire sirens screamed in the distance.

Funny what passes through your mind in an emergency. As I approached the building, running low and fast, I thought about Popper.

She was a pain-in-the-neck third grader who'd befriended us on a case, and we'd been paying for it ever since. She was a loudmouthed, overenthusiastic, triple-talking tree frog.

And she was in trouble.

I leaped directly onto the wall of the burning building.

Not a good idea.

"Whoa! Hot-hot-hot!" I cried, sounding more like Popper than I cared to admit. Scuttling up the wall as quickly as a grasshopper on a griddle, I made straight for the window.

"Here!" shouted Popper. "I'm—*kaffity kaff koff!*—here!"

I reached the windowsill and sucked in a great lungful of smoke. It felt like I'd stuck my head into an

active volcano. The heat swallowed me like a hungry python after a fast.

I hacked and coughed. My eyes watered.

"What—*koff!*—are you—*koff koff!*—stuck on?"

Popper grabbed my shoulder. "This caba-aba-abinet!"

Squinting through the smoke, I could just make out the problem. Popper's face and arms hung out the window, but one leg was pinned to the inside wall by a supply cupboard that had fallen against her.

Oh, boy.

Disobeying my every instinct, I thrust my arms and head into the burning room. I gripped the top of the cabinet, anchored my feet against the outside wall, and pushed.

It didn't budge.

"Kick your—*koff!*—leg, peewee!" I said. "One . . . two . . . *koff koff koff!*"

She kicked, I shoved, and at last the tall cabinet tilted back enough for Popper to snatch her leg out from under.

Whump! The cupboard thunked back against the wall. Flames licked up its side, dancing nearer.

Yikes.

Popper dove out the window.

Time for this detective to make like a grocery checker and bag it.

I tried to squirm backwards, but I felt weaker than a kitten's threat.

"Unh! Aargh!" I thrashed around. My head was spinning. Too much smoke.

A deafening wail tore at my ears. Were my classmates mourning the end of Chet Gecko?

Then, suddenly . . .

"Oof!" Something yanked on my feet and lifted me out. And . . .

Sprisssssh! Jets of water blasted like rap music in a rain barrel. A burly bobcat in a yellow firefighter's jacket hauled Popper and me away from the flames and across the grass.

She propped us against a wall by the crowd of onlookers and headed back to work the hoses. A team of firefighters was drenching every building in sight.

Golden flames sizzled out. Everything reeked of smoke.

"Too bad I—*koff!*—didn't bring ingredients for s'mores," I said.

"*Kaff!* M-m-marshmallowy goodness," said Popper.

For some reason, this struck me funny. My lip twitched. A chuckle erupted, and soon Popper and I were giggling together like fools.

Must have been the smoke inhalation.

Natalie landed beside us in a flurry. "Chet! Are you all right?"

"I—*hee, hee, hee!* I—*ha!*" Laughs kept bursting out of me like cricket popcorn in a skillet.

She scowled. "It's not funny! You could've been fricasseed. What were you doing in there?"

I waved my hand at Popper and the building. "*Ha, ha*—rescue—*hee*—mission."

The tree frog recovered first. "I went in to get my coo-caw-cousin's—*ha*—bracelet. She forgidetty-got it."

"And then?" asked Natalie.

Popper hopped to her feet, vibrating like a paint mixer. "The classroom burn-baby-burned!"

Natalie leaned closer. "Did you see anyone suspicious? Someone who might have set the fire?"

"Yep, yup, uh-huh," said Popper, wiping a smear of soot from her forehead.

I jumped up, shocked sober. "Well? Who was it?"

Popper's mouth dropped open. She pointed across the grass. "Her-her-her."

"Who, her?" I said.

"Maureen De-bubba-Bree!"

10

Sick and Fired

I gasped like a trout tourist in the Painted Desert. "Ms. DeBree?!"

"Are you *sure?*" asked Natalie.

The little tree frog shrugged and nodded and blinked. "Yup, yeah, yo! At least I think, I think so."

"Reeeally?" rumbled a deep voice.

I looked up.

Principal Zero loomed over us. His whiskers bristled. His fangs flashed. He didn't look like a *nice kitty-kitty*.

I gripped Popper's arms. "Are you *absolutely* dead certain?"

The frog shrugged again. "I only saw her from behee-behind the backside, but . . . longity-long tail,

64

brown fur, and criss-cross-criss thingies." Popper pointed at Ms. DeBree's bandoliers full of cleaning products. "And she was bow-bow-bow-bounding away, lickety-split."

"That's all I need to know," said Mr. Zero. "Come with me, Miss LaFrogg."

He plucked Popper from my grasp and steered her over to where Ms. DeBree was talking with the firefighters.

"Uh-oh," said Natalie.

"You can say that again."

"Uh-oh, squared."

"That'll do." I bit my lip and watched the heated conversation between principal and janitor.

By this time, the fire was mostly out. A few tendrils of smoke rose from the half-burned building. Kids and teachers looked on, waiting for the next disaster.

And I had a sinking feeling I knew what that would be.

"Come on," I told Natalie.

We reached Principal Zero and Ms. DeBree just as the fire chief called out, "Hey!" He held up a buckled, blackened thing in his glove. "Think we found what started it. Cleaning solvent—highly flammable."

"That's it!" growled Mr. Zero at the mongoose. "You're fired! No, not just fired, you're under arrest!"

His tail bristled like an electrified pinecone.

"You can't fire me!" cried Ms. DeBree, eyes blazing. "I quit! It's plain as the noise on my face: You're trying for blame me for everything wrong at this school!"

"Take her away!" snapped the principal.

Two dogs in blue cop uniforms stepped forward and seized the mongoose. "Come along, you."

Ms. DeBree searched the faces of the crowd. "I'm innocent, I telling you. Innocent as a lamp."

"That's *lamb*," I muttered.

"Chet!" The janitor reached out a paw. "Help me—prove I didn't do it!"

I swallowed hard. "Popper *saw* you. It doesn't look good."

Ms. DeBree's eyes widened. "What? I never was there! I was fixin' the girls' bathroom sink." As the cops hauled her off, her cries grew fainter. "Ask anybody! Chet! Natalie!"

Principal Zero turned to glare. "You will *not* try to prove she's innocent," he growled. "You will keep your nose to yourself, Gecko—something you desperately need to practice."

I gave him my Bambi-eyed "Who, me?" expression.

Mr. Zero snorted, pointed a claw at me, and then padded over to talk with the firefighters.

Natalie and I gazed at the distant Ms. DeBree. Could Popper and Mr. Dooty have been right?

"Could our janitor really be that sloppy?" I said.

"Or that evil?" said Natalie.

I looked at her; she looked at me. We shook our heads.

"But I see-saw her!" said Popper, bouncing up and down.

I'd forgotten all about the munchkin. (Hard to imagine, I know.) "Tell us everything again," I said. "Slowly."

"Okey-dokey-dokey," said the frog. "I was hippety-hopping down the—"

But just then, the all-clear bell rang.

"Back to class, students!" shouted Principal Zero. "Nothing to see here."

Popper shrugged three times. "Sorry, Chet and Nat, Nat and Chet. Gotta go, go, go! Thanks for saving my lee-lo-life!"

"Can you talk to us after school?" I asked.

The tree frog shook her head so fast, it blurred. "No, nope, *nyet*. I've got studity-student council. See ya tomorrow a.m. in the morning!" And she bounded off like a perpetual motion experiment gone screwy.

"You're not planning to keep investigating after Mr. Zero told you not to?" Natalie asked. "Are you?"

"Do I look like the kind of PI who would ignore a direct order from his principal?"

She cocked her head. "Yes, come to think of it, you do look a lot like Chet Gecko."

"Birdie, you know me too well."

Soaked and smoky, I joined the tide of kids heading back to class.

Mr. Zero was right. I did need practice minding my own beeswax. But then, what card-carrying detective doesn't?

11

Alibi, Bye, Baby

After school, Natalie and I set about proving Ms. DeBree's alibi for the fire. I figured it shouldn't be too hard. I mean, how can you miss a bushy-tailed mongoose fixing a sink?

None of the teachers near the bathrooms remembered seeing her at recess. None of the bathrooms Natalie checked showed any signs of sink repair. But that didn't mean much. Our janitor *was* the queen of clean, after all.

We stopped by the custodian's office to talk with Mr. Dooty. The gopher was out.

"Nothing but dead ends," said Natalie.

"Like kids sitting through a four-hour assembly on a concrete floor," I said.

The school was emptying out. Soon there'd be no one around to investigate. We strode up the halls, hoping for a little blind luck.

What we got was a blind corner.

I rounded the edge of a building and ran straight into Mr. Dooty, hurrying along with his head down. We both staggered back.

"Excuse you, you didn't see me," I said.

"Sure, run me down," he said. "Everyone else does." The gopher brushed dirt from his paws.

"Do you have a minute?" I asked.

Mr. Dooty rolled his eyes. "Oh, right. I'm suddenly head janitor, and I've got to clean up the whole school by myself and hire an assistant, too. I've got nothing but time."

"That's swell," I said, ignoring his sarcasm. "So, we were wondering, how do you guys get your jobs?"

Mr. Dooty scowled. "The principal hires us. Don't you know diddly?"

The gopher pushed past us and trudged down the hall. We followed.

"Not your job," said Natalie, "your *jobs*. You know, the work assignments?"

"Either we do what we see needs doing, or somebody calls us," he said.

"They call?" I said.

"Yeah, this thing called a telephone. They pick it up and dial *M*."

"M?" said Natalie.

Mr. Dooty shrugged. "For *mongoose*. Kinda dumb, but that's Emerson Hicky for you. Full of little indignities. Like *she's* the only janitor."

He stopped a few steps from his office door. A slim brown weasel leaned on the wall, fiddling with a small gadget.

"Here for the, uh, job interview?" said Jerry Dooty.

The weasel nodded.

I held up a hand. "One last thing: Did someone call in a repair for a sink?"

The janitor turned the doorknob. "Nope. Just get it through your head, kid. The mongoose got sloppy, or worse, and now she's paying the price."

"But—" said Natalie.

"Heck," said Mr. Dooty, "*I'm* paying the price. All this work, and now I've got to interview this guy, too. Come on in," he told the weasel. "Waste some more of my time. Everyone else does."

71

His guest sauntered into the office after Mr. Dooty, flicking his long tail. The door swung shut, leaving us alone in the silent hall.

I scratched my head. "Is it just me, or does this case not make any sense at all?"

Natalie grinned. "It's you. You *often* don't make any sense at all."

"When things get twisty and confusing, you know what *does* make sense?"

"Sugary snacks?" she said.

"At my house," I replied.

A half hour later, we had demolished most of a package of frosted earwig balls and were starting in on the lice-cream sandwiches. Natalie and I sat in my home office, cleverly disguised as a big refrigerator box. (The office was disguised, I mean. Not us.)

"It just doesn't fit together," I said. "Food thefts and fires?"

"Cave-ins and missing cash and big stinks?" said Natalie, grooming a tail feather. "You're right. Maybe it's five different troublemakers and five different cases."

"In that case," I bit into the lice-cream sandwich, "we're—*yum*—in trouble. We're not getting anywhere on any of them."

Natalie pecked at her treat. "But if they *are*

connected, what do all these things have in common?"

I took another bite. "*Mmf,* they make Emerson Hicky a dangerous place to spend the day?"

"Or they give someone money, food, and a school without Ms. DeBree," she said.

"But why single her out?" I said. "What's she ever done to anybody?"

Natalie shrugged. "Busted them for littering?"

"Slapped their wrists for leaving gum under the seat? No, there's something else going on here."

"What?" said Natalie.

"Beats me," I said. "Me detective. Me figure things out as me go along."

Natalie raised an eyebrow. "Detective also flunking grammar?"

"Grammar, shmammar," I said. "Pass me another lice-cream sandwich, and let's get down to some serious thinking."

12

The Da Vinci Toad

The next morning dawned as fresh and sweet as a potato-bug pie right out of the oven. At least I think it did. I dawned grumpy and groggy, so I might not have been seeing straight.

Mornings are murder.

Natalie and I hadn't managed to crack open the case with our superior brainpower the night before. That meant we had to do things the old-fashioned way: running down leads and burning up shoe leather.

"Don't forget, tonight is Parents Night," said my mom as I shuffled out the door.

"Who, me?" I said.

"I can tell from your voice that you'd forgotten."

"You can't tell anything from my voice," I said. "I'm a detective."

I stumbled to school on the early side, hoping to get the lowdown from Popper. Natalie was already waiting by the flagpole, slurping up a worm like a fat spaghetti noodle.

She grinned at me. "You know what the early bird gets," she said.

"Yeah, and she can keep it," I said. "That's why I sleep in—usually."

I surveyed the school entrance. Parents were dropping off children on the front sidewalk, and the kids were rushing through the gate with all the zest and enthusiasm of garden slugs on a salt lick. In another ten minutes or so, class would start.

"Any sign of Popper?" I asked.

Natalie shook her head. "Not a peep."

"Let's go beat the bushes."

We circled the school grounds, keeping a sharp eye out for the hyperactive tree frog. She wasn't at the swings. She wasn't under the scrofulous tree. Popper was proving harder to find than a truant officer's soft spot.

As we were passing the basketball courts, we spotted Miss Warts-a-lot, one of the Dirty Rotten Stinkers. The hefty toad was leaning against a pole, polishing her warts. When she saw us, the Stinker crooked a finger.

"Hey, Gecko," she croaked. "C'mere."

I tipped my hat. "No, thanks. I like my face the way it is."

"Yeah, we've finally gotten used to it," said Natalie.

Miss Warts-a-lot glanced over her shoulder at some nearby sixth graders. "Come closer. The name's Helen Weals. I don't bite."

"Neither does a rattlesnake," I said. "Much."

The toad scowled. "I'm tryin' to do you a favor, buddy. Don't tick me off."

I shifted my weight onto the balls of my feet. "And what kind of favor can a Stinker offer, Miss Weals?"

"Ah, forget you, wise guy," Helen snarled. She pushed off the pole, glanced around again, and then fixed us with a stare. "You don't wanna hear about the missing frog? Fine. But here's one piece of advice."

I couldn't help myself. "Never order the cafeteria's Mystery Meat on a Monday?"

The toad clenched a fist and took a step toward us.

Natalie and I backed up.

Helen stabbed a clawed finger at me. "You, you're too smart for your own good."

"Funny," said Natalie, "but Mr. Ratnose never says that."

"You, too, birdbrain," croaked the toad. "You think you're such hotshot detectives, but the answer to your case is right under—"

Just then, a familiar voice rumbled from off to the side, "Way to go, Helen! Now we got 'em."

A quick glance revealed the cuddly, car-sized tarantula Erik Nidd with the rat Kurt Replie circling behind us.

Helen Weals cleared her throat. "Uh, yeah, you

lousy, uh, peepers. Now you're gonna find yourself in a world of ouchiness!"

Natalie and I turned back-to-back to face the Stinkers. "What's your gripe, Guido?" I asked Erik. "I mean, aside from the usual."

"Ya mean, hatin' the world?" he asked.

"Yeah."

Erik sidled closer. "Well, ya keep stickin' yer nose where it don't belong," he said. "That's a good way to lose it."

I took a step back and bumped into Natalie. "And since when do you care about my nose?"

"Since it got all up in my beeswax," snarled the tarantula. Kurt clenched his paws and stepped to one side, blocking our escape. Helen spread her arms. Erik crawled forward.

Desperate times call for desperate measures.

"Alley-oop on three," I muttered to Natalie. "One..."

"Two...," she said.

"Three!" I cried, taking a step and a hop straight at the huge tarantula.

His mouth hung open in confusion. On him, it looked natural. "Huh?"

"Alley-oop!" I jumped again with all my might, right onto Erik's back.

"Hey!" he bellowed. "Ya can't do that, ya mug!"

I grabbed his two long feelers like ski poles and bent my legs for balance. "Too late," I said. "I done did it."

Erik's front legs waved like a bunch of hairy trolls dancing the Hot Cucamonga. But he couldn't reach me. I kept my feet planted as his back rocked to and fro.

Natalie had taken to the skies and was flapping just above the grasp of Kurt and Helen.

As Erik twisted and struggled, a thought ran through my mind: It's one thing getting *onto* an angry tarantula; it's a whole 'nother thing getting *off*.

The class bell rang.

Like that mattered. The Dirty Rotten Stinkers had about as much use for school rules as a raging bull has for little pink booties. If I didn't find a way off of this thug pronto, I'd soon be gecko sushi.

Round and round Erik whirled. Tighter and tighter I clung to his furry feelers.

"Yow!" he cried. "Easy with them things!"

As he turned, I caught glimpses of empty basketball courts, fresh piles of dirt, and a panting janitor bustling up to us.

"Hey there, you kids," shouted Jerry Dooty. "Knock it off!"

"He started it!" cried Erik.

"Only because *he*"—I tweaked his feeler—"was trying to clobber me."

"Ow!"

The gopher janitor held up his hands. "I don't care who started it. Stop it now!" He glanced over his shoulder and lowered his voice. "You're trying to make me look bad, aren't you?"

I followed his gaze and spotted Principal Zero standing over by the classrooms, arms crossed. Erik noticed him, too.

"Truce?" said the tarantula.

"Truce," I agreed.

I hopped off and stood near the janitor. Erik crawled over to join his pals. Natalie mouthed, "Later," and flew off to class.

"This ain't over, peeper," growled the tarantula.

Jerry Dooty gave him a warning look and a head shake.

The tarantula rolled his many eyes. "Come on, Stinkers," he said. "Let's motorvate."

They swaggered across the grass.

"Mr. Dooty," I said, "you saved my bacon."

He blew out a sigh. "Like I don't have enough on my plate already. Nobody knows how tough this job is. It's thankless, I tell you."

What could I say to that, but "Um, thanks"? Then off I dashed to class.

13

Clue in the Face

I slipped into my seat just as Mr. Ratnose was finishing up roll call.

"*There's* one of our missing members," he said. "Thanks for joining us, Chet Gecko. Now has anyone heard from Rick Shaw? Olive Drabb? Bo Newt?"

My classmates shrugged or shook their heads.

Mr. Ratnose paced. "This is highly irregular. Their parents are going to hear all about it at Parents Night."

Of course, if they were lucky, the kids would miss Parents Night altogether. (Which was far more than *I* could hope for.)

Mr. Ratnose surveyed the classroom. "Hmm," he said.

I knew just how he felt. Something was fishier than an orca's breath at breakfast. But what?

And was it tied into my case or just some random happening?

I watched Mr. Ratnose for a clue, but all he said was "Open your math books to page forty-three." And as clues go, that was pretty disappointing.

The minutes stretched like your mom's oldest swimsuit. It seemed to take a short forever for recess to arrive and another brief eternity until lunch.

After a hurried meal of curried centipede casserole and mayfly salad (with cicada strawberry shortcake for dessert), Natalie and I continued our dogged search for clues, insights, and the elusive thread that would tie everything together.

We found exactly bupkes, zip, nada, and diddly-squat.

Being thorough, we even followed up on Mrs. Crow's lead and talked to the teacher whose building had collapsed. No clues there either.

(Detective work isn't always easy confessions and fat bonuses, you know.)

Natalie and I climbed to the top of the jungle gym to try to get a different angle on things. No luck. The world looked just as confusing from up there.

We saw a group of rodents playing tag, a pair of sixth-grade sweethearts swapping spit, a ragged game of football, and a long-tailed weasel (the new assistant janitor) bounding after three kids who'd overturned a trash can.

The usual lunchtime hijinks.

"That weasel," said Natalie.

"Yeah?"

"Something bugs me about him," she said, cocking her head.

I slowly stood, balancing on the highest bars. "What?"

Natalie cocked her head the other way. "His looks . . . the way he moves . . . I don't know. Does he remind you of anyone?"

My arms windmilled. "Uh, no."

"Aw . . . it's on the tip of my tongue."

"Then spit it out, sister," I said, swaying this way and that, like a politician looking for votes.

Natalie stuck out a wing feather and tickled my toe. That was all it took.

"Hee, hee—yahh!" Down I tumbled into the sand.

Flat on my back, I gazed up through the bars at my partner's face.

"What are we missing?" she asked.

I pulled myself to standing. "Um, a pink Cadillac, a secret hideout, the answers to every test question, a lifelong pass to Dizzyland, the world's biggest mosquito milk shake, and, oh . . . a suspect that ties all these crimes together."

She glided off the jungle gym and landed in the sand. "Exactly. And what did that Stinker, Helen Weals, say?"

"That I was too smart," I said.

"Besides that." Natalie led the way out of the sandbox. "She said the answer was right under . . . something. Our noses?"

"Our armpits?"

As if we had conjured them up, three of the Dirty Rotten Stinkers appeared across the playground. They snatched a little shrew and dragged him back into the shadows of the nearest building, no doubt to "borrow" his pocket money.

The *shadows* . . .

"I have a thought," I said.

"Better give it to me," said Natalie. "You're not used to taking care of them."

I ambled across the grass, mulling things over. "Something is definitely going on at this school."

"As the wise man said, 'No duh.' "

"And I'll bet you dollars to doughnuts it's going on when nobody is looking," I said. "In the dark. After hours."

Natalie eyed me. "Okay . . ."

"So *that's* when we need to be here."

She stopped. "You mean tonight?"

I nodded. "Tonight."

"But tonight is Parents Night. We need to be here anyway."

"There you go," I said. "Am I not brilliant, or am I not brilliant?"

"Chet," said Natalie.

"Yeah?" I said.

"You're not brilliant."

14

Charge of the Night Brigade

That evening, the school was lit up like Grandma Gecko's birthday cake. Doors dripped with colorful student artwork. Kids roamed about. Parents said embarrassing things and practiced strange contortions to sit in their kids' chairs.

Normally I would've found this scene a barrel of yuks. Normally my school wasn't falling apart, thanks to some nutcase on a rampage.

I gave my parents the slip as they went in to hobnob with my sister Pinky's teacher.

"We'll meet you at Mr. Ratnose's class in twenty minutes," called Ma Gecko.

My father just rolled his eyes. He knew how my parent-teacher visits usually turned out.

"And don't forget!" said Pinky.

I gave her the traditional brotherly salute: one tongue, sticking straight out.

Only twenty minutes. And I had to make each one count.

Natalie was waiting near her classroom. "The clock is ticking," she said. "So, where to, Mr. PI?"

I bit my lip, deciding. "The cafeteria."

She smirked. "Big surprise there."

"Not for food," I said, hotfooting it down the halls. "To answer a question that's been bugging me."

"You mean, 'Why is Natalie so much smarter than me?'"

"No, birdbrain. 'How did the thieves get in to steal the food?'"

We rounded the corner and approached the cafeteria. I tried the kitchen door. Locked. We made a full circuit of the building. No secret passages revealed themselves. No broken windows gaped.

"Okay, I give up," said Natalie. "How *did* they get in?"

I straightened my hat. "Let's go inside and find out."

We slipped into the auditorium, where Mrs. Bagoong had laid out cookies and other treats for the horde of visiting parents. One or two blister-beetle brownies found their way into my pockets as we passed. (Okay, three or four.)

Nobody paid any mind as we made our way back into the dim kitchen. Methodically, I paced through the room, tapping on walls and feeling for hidden catches.

"Remind me again," said Natalie, "why we're here, when the culprit could be anywhere at school, stirring up trouble?"

I lifted a shoulder. "Just a hunch," I said. "Maybe they'll return."

"For more food?" Natalie said.

"Mmm." I reached into my pocket, pulled out a brownie, and bit off a chunk. The pantry door was slightly ajar, so I nudged it open.

"Just because *you're* a bottomless pit doesn't mean the thief is," said Natalie.

I took a step into the darkened pantry. "Hey, I'm just a growing gecko with—"

But I never did finish that sentence. Instead, I stepped into thin air and fell, whacking my head on the edge of the hole and vanishing into the earth.

Whump! I belly flopped hard, knocking the wind out of me.

"Chet?" Natalie's voice came from above. "What are you—"

I tried to warn her, but could only whisper.

Thump! Natalie landed smack on my back, smashing me flatter than Darth Vader's fan-mail file.

"Oof," I wheezed.

She bounced to her feet. "You could've at least given me a heads-up."

With Natalie's help, I sat and looked around.

We found ourselves in a low-ceilinged tunnel, lit with strings of Christmas lights. Sort of a festive secret passage. It smelled overpoweringly of fresh earth, like the assembly line at a mud pie factory.

"Wow." I patted the ladder that led up into the pantry. "No wonder he could rob the cafeteria so easily."

Natalie whistled. "Pretty slick for an underground highway."

I got to my feet and started down the passage. "Wonder where this goes . . ."

"Do you think it's safe?" asked Natalie.

"No," I said. "But if we wanted safe, we should've become cheese testers. Come on."

Carefully, we crept onward, hugging the wall. The tunnel was quieter than a king snake in a snowbank. Before long, we reached another ladder, which led up to a trapdoor.

Muffled voices and crowlike squawks drifted through the floor.

"The office," I whispered. Natalie nodded.

We resumed our trek through the tunnel. It began sloping downward, and the farther we went, the

colder it got. Two smaller tunnels fed into it from the left, but we stuck with the main passage.

"Just think of all the burrowing it took," said Natalie. "That's a lot of earth to move."

I grinned. "I can dig it."

She groaned. "This explains all the dirt piles around the playground."

Natalie brushed the wall with a wing tip as we walked down, down, down. "Must have taken more than just one bad guy to do all this burrowing."

"Unless we're talking about one monster-sized earthworm," I said.

"Mmm," said Natalie dreamily. "Giant worms."

But I didn't get the chance to hear about her food fantasies. Because just then, we rounded a bend in the tunnel and saw its destination.

"Holy mole, Batman," breathed Natalie.

"You ain't a-woofin', sister," I said.

The tunnel ended at the lip of a crater. Stretching below and above was a huge cavern, lit with spotlights and dangling Christmas bulbs. Somewhere nearby, a generator rumbled.

"This explains the extra-high electricity bill," I said.

Small, round doors studded the sides of the cavern, all around. And way out in the middle, a huge earthen throne arose.

"Look!" said Natalie.

Kids labored below us, lugging buckets. I spotted Popper, Bo Newt, and about a dozen other students, all handcuffed to a ladder and dragging it by their ankles.

"This is either Santa's dirt workshop," I said, "or the winter palace of the Worm King."

"Wrong on both counts, peeper," growled a familiar voice.

And up over the lip of the cavern crawled Erik Nidd.

15

The Hole Thing

"**E**rik!" I said, backing up. "I never figured you for a tunnel spider."

His fangs glistened in a wicked smile. "Ya never figured on a lot, shamus."

Natalie and I edged back into the tunnel as Erik, the rat Kurt Replie, the ferret Bosco Rebbizi, and our old friend the eggplant-nosed mole climbed up onto our level. My tail bumped against some empty buckets.

"*You're* behind it all?" I said to the tarantula. "The stealing, the burning—"

"The cave-in," said Natalie.

"*That* was a mistake," snapped Eggplant Nose. "*Somebody* didn't follow my digging instructions."

Bosco waved a finger at the mole. "And *somebody* forgot that I'm a ferret, not a prairie dog."

"So *you're* behind it all?" I asked Eggplant Nose, slipping my tail through the bucket handles.

"Pal, you are *way* too curious," he said. "That's gonna land you in real trouble one of these days."

I gave him a friendly grin. "Like now?" In a flash, I whipped my tail and slung the buckets straight into the thugs.

The Stinkers staggered back, disoriented.

Natalie and I whirled around and beat feet.

"Snatch 'em, boys!" cried the mole.

The gang gave a yell. Footsteps thundered behind us.

We pounded up the passageway with the bullies in hot pursuit. Round the twists and turns we went, higher and higher. Somehow, we carved out a lead.

But the tunnel was a lot trickier going uphill. My legs grew heavier than a cheater's conscience. My lungs burned. Soon I was panting like a black dog on a summer day.

Natalie and I rounded a corner. The first side passage lay just ahead, and the Stinkers were still out of sight.

"Quick!" I hissed. "In here!"

I took off my hat and flung it farther up the main tunnel. Then we dove into the smaller passage and scrambled up it.

Natalie and I pressed ourselves to the wall. I tried to quiet my steam-train breathing and slow my drum-soloing heart.

Behind us, muffled voices echoed.

"This way!" said Erik. "That's Gecko's hat."

Their footsteps thudded on.

I exhaled. Natalie gave me a shaky thumbs-up.

"Wait," said Bosco's distant voice. "They're just the kind of low-down sneaks that would try to give us the slip." Footsteps padded closer.

I shot a worried look at Natalie.

"I smell fresh gecko!" cried Bosco, his voice suddenly loud. "Up here!"

Natalie and I hightailed it. The side tunnel narrowed and rose. After another minute of full-tilt running, we turned a bend.

I stopped short. Natalie piled into me.

"Dead end?!" she said.

The passage sloped up sharply into the ceiling. My scrabbling hands touched wood.

"Another trapdoor." I put my shoulder to it. "Push, Natalie!"

We shoved, hard. It didn't budge.

The Dirty Rotten Stinkers rounded the final corner and spotted us.

"Hah!" cried Erik. "Say your prayers, Gecko."

The bullies rolled forward slowly, deliberately, smiling evil smiles.

"Push harder!" I cried.

And with one last "*Oof!*" we slammed the trapdoor back on its hinges, tumbling out into . . .

The janitor's office?

Jerry Dooty slumped on a stool just above us, staring down with his mournful eyes.

"Mr. Dooty," said Natalie. "Help us!"

We scrambled to our feet.

"Another problem for my to-do list?" he whined. "What is it this time?"

Bosco's head and shoulders emerged from the trapdoor. "They saw our operations, boss."

The gopher sighed. "My, that *is* a problem."

"*Boss?*" I said.

Jerry Dooty grinned and picked up a fancy golden crown from the table. "I prefer 'All-Powerful Emperor of the Underground,'" he said. "But 'boss' is a start."

16

Dooty Calls

My brain felt like a locomotive that had piled into a Jell-O mountain. The wheels were spinning, but I couldn't get any traction.

"You *huh?*" I said. "You *whuh?*"

The gopher *tsk-tsk*ed. "Really, I would've thought a detective would be a little sharper than that. Yes, I'm the genius behind it all."

"*You?*" said Natalie.

Jerry Dooty placed the crown on his head. "What, you don't think I'm smart enough?" He pouted. "Nobody ever does. I'm *so* unappreciated, even as an emperor."

"But . . . *emperor?*" I said.

"Yes," said the gopher. "I'm tired of the way things are run around here."

"Us, too," said Erik, peeking up through the hole in the floor.

Mr. Dooty gestured to the trapdoor. "So I decided to create my own underground empire, with a little help from my minions. Like it?"

Natalie and I exchanged a quick glance.

"Yeah, it's, uh, swell," I said.

"Especially the twinkly lights," Natalie added.

The janitor nodded. "Thanks. I wanted it to be cheery."

My stunned gaze wandered around the room, from the deranged gopher, to the bottles of cleaning products, to the Stinkers peering up through the floor.

"So you got Ms. DeBree fired?" I said. "Why?"

"She was just too darn clean," said the janitor.

I blinked. "How's that?"

He waved a paw. "Always tidying things up, poking her nose into stuff. She was getting suspicious. Maureen could have derailed my whole plan."

Natalie shifted from foot to foot. She cut her eyes at the trapdoor and floor bolt, then back to me. I gave a tiny nod.

"One thing I don't get," she said. "Popper saw Ms. DeBree running away just before that building caught fire."

"Hah!" said Erik. "Should I tell 'em, boss?"

"That's *emperor*," said Jerry Dooty.

"*I'll* tell them," a new voice cut in.

I turned to see the weasel assistant janitor pushing through the office door. "You!"

"Yes," he said, tossing a lighter from paw to paw.

"Funny how from behind, a weasel looks just like a mongoose."

Natalie snapped her forefeathers. "I *knew* there was something odd about him."

"His bad-guy vibes?" I said.

"No, the way he moves," she said. "Mongooses dash, weasels bound. And Popper said the culprit bow-bow-bounded away. So it couldn't have been a mongoose."

I shook my head. "You spend *way* too much time watching the Natural Channel. But good work, partner."

Bosco the ferret raised a paw. "'Scuse me, boss—"

"Emperor!" snapped Mr. Dooty.

"—but are we gonna stand around jawing all night, or are we gonna chain these two up on the work crew?"

The janitor adjusted his crown. "Excellent idea, minion."

"The name's not Minion," said Bosco. "It's Bosco."

They glared at each other. The weasel kept on tossing his lighter.

Natalie threw me another sharp look and cut her eyes back to the open trapdoor. "Now!" she cried.

Together we sprang for the door, lifted it, and slammed it—*thonk!*—right onto the heads of the Dirty Rotten Stinkers.

Muffled *ow*s rose through the floor as I snapped the bolt home, locking the bullies below.

"Hey!" said Emperor Dooty. "That's not fair!"

With my quick gecko reflexes, I snatched the lighter from the weasel, mid-throw. "Neither is *this*, but I'm doing it anyway."

I grabbed the nearest jar marked FLAMMABLE, unscrewed the lid, and held the lighter near it.

"You wouldn't," said the weasel.

"Just try me, Sparky," I said, backing toward the exit.

Natalie slipped around me and went to the door. "Stand back, or you'll find out who *else* around here can play with fire."

The pyro weasel eased off to stand beside the janitor.

"You are a dead lizard," growled Jerry Dooty.

"You should know about dead," I said. "Because, judging by your breath, something died in your mouth."

I managed a cocky chuckle, but I just knew my parents would kill me if they found out about this.

Natalie opened the door. I backed through it, still holding the lighter and the solvent.

"Sayonara, nutbags!" I said.

Wham! Natalie slammed the door, I tossed the lighter and cleaning fluid into the bushes, and we screamed out of there like a kindergartner with a brand-new trike.

Parents and kids stared as we blew past.

Fhomp! The janitor's door banged open behind us. I risked a glance back.

Emperor Dooty and his minions spilled into the hall. The gopher took in all the witnesses. With both hands, he made a *keep cool* gesture to his crew.

The Stinkers and Pyro Weasel chased us at a fast walk. "Just a game," called the weasel to the parents. "Heh-heh. No reason for alarm."

Sure. And if you believe that one, I've got some beachfront property for you at the North Pole.

Natalie and I poured on the gas—me running, her flying. We blew past a classroom door. "Chet!" someone called.

"I think that was your teacher," said Natalie.

Pumping my arms, I panted, "I'll save my grade after I save my skin."

I kept my eyes peeled for Mr. Zero, Vice Principal Shrewer, or any teacher with enough clout to stop Mad Emperor Dooty. The last person I expected to see was Maureen DeBree.

And yet, as we veered around a corner, there she was.

"Hey, the private eyeballs!" said Ms. DeBree. She wore a blond wig and floppy hat, but I'd have recognized that mongoose mug anywhere. Definitely not a weasel.

I skidded to a halt. "Why the weird getup?"

"Disguise," she said. "I like find some evidence and clear my name. Where you off to?"

"No time to explain."

She blew wig hairs away from her mouth. "Try anyhow."

"Bad gopher. Dug tunnels. Got you fired. Wants to be underground emperor."

Natalie landed on a nearby bush. "Guess there *was* time after all."

I glanced behind us. No Stinkers yet, but they wouldn't be long.

"Hurry!" I said. "How do we stop him?"

The mongoose smiled a crafty smile. "Where's the bugger got his tunnel entrances at?"

17

Fine Feathered Ends

In three shakes of a gecko's tail, we were standing outside the administration office. Ms. DeBree held a thick green hose with a spray-nozzle gizmo at the end. Jerry Dooty and his crew strode up the hall with bloody murder in their eyes.

The mongoose stepped to the door, hose in hand.

"Where do you think you're going?" called Emperor Dooty.

"To clean up after you," said Ms. DeBree.

"Talk about a full-time job," I muttered.

I turned the knob, and we stepped inside. Principal Zero stood talking with several parents in the hall outside his office. He raised a bristly eyebrow.

"Don't mind us," said Natalie.

She and I dropped to the floor and began tapping the tiles.

"Excuse me?" said the secretary, Mrs. Crow.

"You're excused," I said.

Mr. Zero broke away from his conference. "Gecko, what is the meaning of this?" Then he caught sight of the ex-janitor. "You? I fired you!"

"We came for flush out one dirty rotten gopher," said Ms. DeBree.

I kept tapping. "Jerry Dooty is behind everything. The fire, the stinkbomb, the building collapse . . ."

"The thefts and the disappearing kids," said Natalie.

The gopher burst through the doorway. "Lies! All madness and lies!"

Mr. Zero looked from him to us. Hard to say who looked crazier—Maureen DeBree with her wig, hat, and hose, or Jerry Dooty in his crooked crown.

The big cat turned to Natalie. "Miss Attired, you're usually saner than your partner."

"Hey!" I said.

"Tell me what's going on here."

Natalie thumped the floor. "Mr. Dooty tunneled under the whole school—even this office. That's how he stole things; that's why the classroom caved in."

"Ridiculous!" scoffed Emperor Dooty. "Who will

you believe—your head custodian, or a couple of cockamamie kids and an ex-employee with a grudge?"

"Well . . . ," said Mr. Zero, undecided.

I kept thumping.

"Tunnels under the floor?" said Pyro Weasel over Mr. Dooty's shoulder. "Preposterous!"

Just when I was about to give up, one tile gave a hollow *tonk!* "Help me, birdie," I said.

Working together, Natalie and I pried up the trapdoor and let it fall open.

"Preposterous?" said Mr. Zero.

Mr. Dooty turned pale. "I've never seen that hole before."

Maureen DeBree stepped up to the tunnel entrance. The hose was so full of backed-up water, she had to wrestle it under control. "Okeydokey," she said. "Then you won't mind if we . . ." She lowered the nozzle into the opening.

At that moment, I heard children's voices below us. An image sprang to my mind: helpless kids, handcuffed to a ladder.

Time slowed down.

The mongoose's fingers tightened on the trigger. I reached for her arm, but before I could speak . . .

"Wait!" cried Mr. Dooty. "Don't—there's kids down there!"

"Kids?" said the principal.

We leaned over the hole. Below us, dirty faces looked up. "Hippety-hi-hi-hi, Chet," said Popper.

Mr. Zero's eyes went wider than the waistband of an elephant's undies. "They're cuffed together? To our good ladder? Get that hose out of here!"

Ms. DeBree hauled it back out. "Sorry, eh," she said. "I just wanted for expose *his* evil—" She gestured at Jerry Dooty with the hose.

Psssshhht! A supercharged stream of water blasted from the nozzle and hit the gopher smack-dab in the chest.

Foom! Down he went like a greenhorn tightrope walker, taking out the weasel and one or two Stinkers with him.

"Oops," said Ms. DeBree. "Clumsy me."

Before long, Mr. Zero had sorted out the whole mess like a—well, like an espresso-fueled janitor on a cleaning binge. He hauled up the captive kids and uncuffed them, and ordered the new-old head custodian, Maureen DeBree, to plug up the tunnel pronto.

The boys in blue roared into the parking lot, sirens wailing. They hauled off Jerry Dooty and his crew in the paddy wagon—even the Dirty Rotten Stinkers. Bo, Popper, and the other former captives stood at the curb, cheering.

Natalie and I watched the van drive away. The crowd slowly dispersed.

I kicked at a weed sticking up through the pavement.

"For a gecko who just helped stop an evil emperor and save some kidnapped kids, you don't look too happy," said Natalie.

I sighed. "Ah, it's just that . . . I was wrong all the way down the line."

"What do you mean?" she asked.

"I had no clue who was behind it all, I nearly got us thrown on the chain gang . . . Heck, without Ms. DeBree, I wouldn't even have been able to get those guys locked up." I hugged my arms. "Some detective I am."

Natalie patted my shoulder. "Relax, Chet. You always goof up."

"Thanks a lot."

"But you always get there in the end."

I trudged down the sidewalk. "I dunno, birdie. Maybe the time has come to hang up the old trench coat."

Natalie frowned. "What are you saying?"

"Time to quit being a PI."

She stopped dead. "You? Quit detective work? You're kidding."

"I'm as serious as a ten-page math test." I rubbed my neck. "Time for me to focus on being a regular kid. You know—do homework, bring my grades up, do chores around the house."

For a long moment, I stared at Natalie. She stared right back at me.

"Nah," we said together. "It'd never work."

Natalie punched my arm. "Besides, who's the school's best lizard detective?"

"Me?" I said.

"Right as usual, Sherlock. Sharpest mind in the business."

Just then, a voice rang out from behind us. "Chet Gecko! Did you forget something?"

I turned to see Mr. Ratnose and my parents standing by the office.

"My reward?" I said.

"Your parent-teacher conference," said Mr. Ratnose.

Natalie smirked. "Like I said, sharpest mind in the business."

BRUCE HALE is the author of fifteen Chet Gecko mysteries, as well as *Snoring Beauty,* illustrated by Howard Fine. A popular speaker, teacher, and storyteller for children and adults, he lives in Santa Barbara, California.

www.brucehale.com

More funny fiction

Whales on Stilts
By M. T. Anderson

The Clue of the Linoleum Lederhosen
By M. T. Anderson

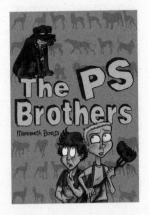

The PS Brothers
By Maribeth Boelts

Thor's Wedding Day
By Bruce Coville

The Neddiad
By Daniel Pinkwater

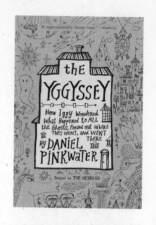

The Yggysey
By Daniel Pinkwater

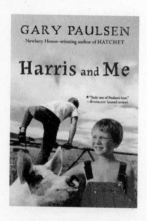

Harris and Me
By Gary Paulsen

**Max Quigley,
Technically Not a Bully**
By James Roy

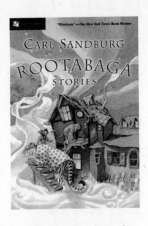

Rootabaga Stories
By Carl Sandburg

Smart Dog
By Vivian Vande Velde

Detectives in Togas
By Henry Winterfeld

**Mystery of the
Roman Ransom**
By Henry Winterfeld

The Magic Shop Books
By Bruce Coville

The Starbuck Twins Mysteries

By Kathryn Lasky

Regarding the . . . series

By Kate Klise
Illustrated by M. Sarah Klise

Secrets of Dripping Fang series

By Dan Greenberg